THIS BOOK BELONGS TO

....

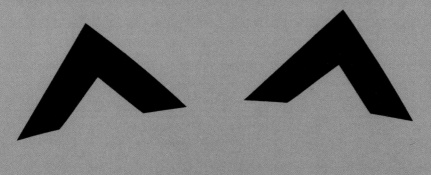

On a crisp autumn morning, Logan wandered through the forest. He took a long walk to his friend's house. As he came closer, he noticed that there was something different.

Violet was decorating her den; she was placing lights and other decorations outside her house.

"What are you doing?" asked Logan with confusion. He had never seen Violet do this before.

"Oh, Hello, Topsy! Do you know what Halloween is?"
Logan asked.

"Of course! "Topsy lowered his voice and bellowed "It's the night of horror, muah ha ha!!!"

"So, we scare everyone?" Logan said.

Topsy laughed, "Yes, we dress up first. I have a few costumes. Guess you'll want to try them on?"

He tried on lots of different costumes.

His favorite was the long silky cloak with a bow tie.

Topsy gave him fake red fangs and some
white face paint to complete the look.
Then Topsy went in to get ready.

Topsy and Logan were both ready for Halloween.
After the sun had set, they headed out excitedly
eager to show off their costumes.

Violet was surprised, "I didn't even recognize you both!" She exclaimed.

"Happy Halloween!" Logan said in a deep voice.

Logan, Topsy, and Violet went to see the twins, Cole and Angie.
They wanted to celebrate Halloween together.

Cole and Angie looked terrifying!

"So, what do we do at Halloween?" Logan whispered to Topsy.

"Pumpkin carving!" Topsy replied.

"Yes, let's carve pumpkins and make lanterns out of them. It can be a competition! We can take our pumpkins to Mendal. He can decide who the winner is." Cole suggested.

The dinosaurs got to work. Violet grew pumpkins in her garden, so there was plenty to go around.

She gave all of her friends one pumpkin.
They used their sharp teeth to carve.

Topsy carved a skull;

Logan made a face with razor-sharp teeth;

Cole's pumpkin only had one eye!

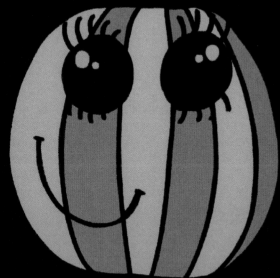

Violets pumpkin was more cute than scary,

and Angie's pumpkin was very odd indeed.

They lit all the pumpkins up and then walked towards mount Ivius, where Mendal the wisest dinosaur of all lived. They scared the other dinosaurs and animals along the way.

"Happy Halloween!" They all cheered together.

"Happy Halloween, little dinosaurs!" Mendal replied with happiness. "Those are some scary looking pumpkins," he added.

"It was a competition. Who do you think did the best?" Violet asked.

Mendal loved Angie's pumpkin with the weird face. "They are all fantastic, but in all my years, I have never seen a face as scary as that!"

"Yay! Now, let's go trick or treating!" said Angie.

"Trick or treat?"

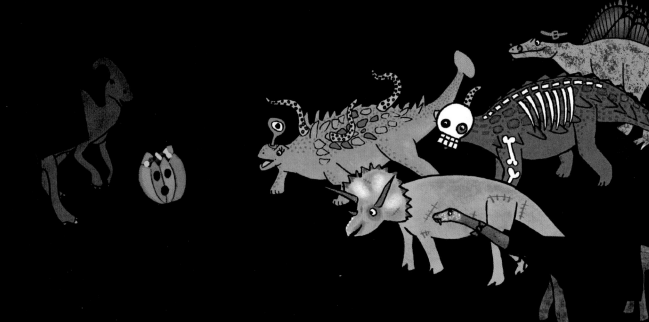

They spent a couple of hours going
around the jungle collecting treats from
the other animals and dinosaurs.

They were all exhausted. Collecting candy is quite tiring after all. Luckily, when they returned, Mendal had already prepared a Halloween Feast.

The dinosaurs sat around the campfire, sharing treats and scary stories. It was Mendal's turn to tell his tale.

"Once upon a time, there was a large ferocious monster called Frodagg. He would wander through the forest and snack on little dinosaurs. Defeating him seemed like an impossible task.

A group of little dinosaurs tried their hardest means to stop him. They thought they had finally captured the terrifying beast, but he escaped! It would only be a matter of time until he would return...

"They should have defeated him. That's not a happily ever after kind of ending!" Said Cole.

"Oh! but it is, these little dinosaurs were not upset because they didn't capture Frodagg. They knew the secret. Another wise old dinosaur once told me, "The greatest test of our courage on earth is to bear defeat without losing heart."

"What does that mean exactly?" Asked Topsy with a mouth full of chocolate.

"Sometimes you win, and sometimes you learn" shouted Violet.

"Exactly Violet, we learn from our mistakes. We keep learning and growing.

Mistakes are superpowers because they can help you turn into something better than you were before."

"Wow, you are right Mendal, I never thought of it that way." Said Cole

"I am always right," joked Mendal.

The dinosaurs chuckled; the sugar crash had begun. They closed their eyes and started to drift off. What a marvellous Halloween they had. Pumpkins, feasts, Scary Stories, Costumes, Trick or treating, and candy! What more could they ask for?

THE END.

13188041R00021

Made in the
USA
Monee, IL